Library of Congress Cataloging-in-Publication Data is available.

ISBN 13: 978-1-935954-05-7 (Hardcover)

Printing and binding: Worzalla, Stevens Point, WI

TOM THE TAMER

Tjibbe Veldkamp en Philip Hopman

One day Tom cobbled together a trampoline for the snails in the garden.

As soon as the snails had learned a few simple jumps, Tom yelled: 'Hey Dad!

The show is starting! Come see!'

His father didn't come.

Tom clambered up his tree and made trapezes for the squirrels.

As soon as the squirrels came gliding by, Tom yelled:

'Hey Dad! The squirrel circus is in town! Come see!'

His father didn't come.

Tom's father stayed indoors all the time. There
were animals outside, and animals terrified him.
Often Tom had asked him: 'What animals
scare you?'

'Butterflies for example,' his father said.

'But they don't harm anyone,' said Tom.

'Yes they do!' his father said. 'Butterflies are
dangerous. And snails and even more so,
squirrels!'

Nothing helped … whatever Tom said. His
father remained afraid and stayed inside. And
that's why Tom thought up a new show.

He went to the 'Paws, Claws, Beaks & Bugs' pet store in town.

'I am Tom the Tamer,' he said. 'By any chance do you have a couple
of animals that still need to be tamed?'

'What kind of animal did you have in mind?' asked the storekeeper.

'A hamster? Or perhaps a small dog?'

'I was thinking of a polar bear,' said Tom.

'Polar animals are in the back,' said the man. 'Come this way ...

Then you can select one.'

Tom tamed the polar bear in the park.

Then Tom told him about the new show.

The polar bear was happy to join in.

'What would you like to be?' Tom asked.

The polar bear sat down and tucked-in his head.

'Cool!' cried Tom. 'I can see what you're being.'

That night a large white comfy chair was sitting in the house.

Tom's father looked at it from all sides.

'That chair...' he said. 'I never knew we had that?'

'It's a new one,' said Tom.

'It's a little bit furry,' said Tom's father. 'Other chairs aren't half as furry.'

'That's why this chair is so much nicer,' said Tom. 'Try it!'

Tom's father carefully sat down in the chair.

'Ah...' he sighed. 'It feels divine.'

The chair winked at Tom and Tom winked back.

The next day Tom and the polar bear went back to the 'Paws,
Claws, Beaks & Bugs' pet store. There they picked up a whole
bunch of animals. Tom tamed them, and the polar bear told
them about the show. All the animals wanted to join in.

That afternoon the house was full of new stuff.
The show had begun.

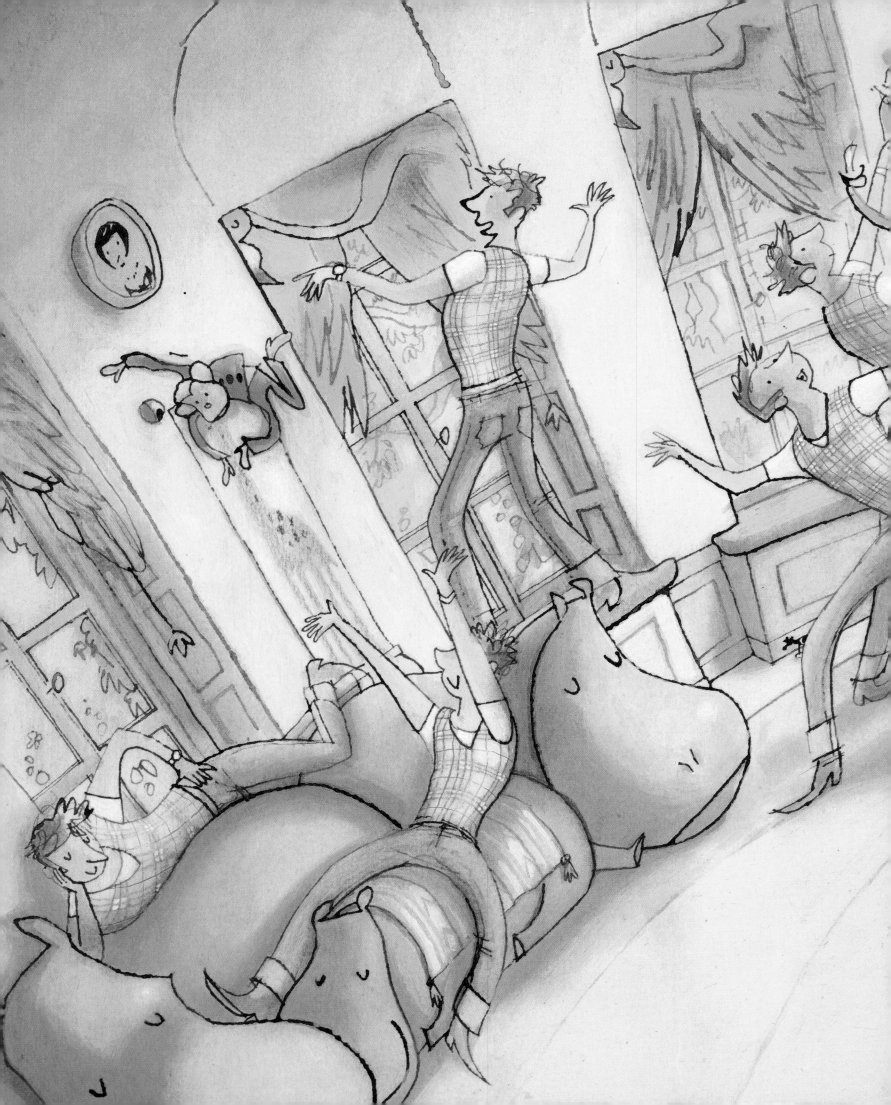

Tom's father was astonished. He walked from the new carpet to the new lamp; from the new lamp to the new couch; from the new couch along the new curtains and the new table to the new paintings and back. And everything was touched, tried and tested.

Finally Tom's father flopped into
the white comfy chair.
'There's one thing I am not getting
though,' he said. 'Where did all
this stuff come from?'
'From the 'Paws, Claws, Beaks &
Bugs,' pet store said Tom.
'What?' cried Tom's father. 'You
brought something home from a
pet store?'
'A tiger, an octopus, a tortoise, a
snake, two peacocks, three hippos
and three flamingos,' Tom listed.
'And the polar bear you're sitting
on.'
'A tiger, an octopus, a tortoise, a
snake, two peacocks, three hippos
and three flamingos?' exclaimed
Tom's father. 'And I'm sitting on a
polar bear?' …
He flew out of his chair.

And all the animals bowed since the show was over.
'Cool!' yelled Tom.

'Help!' cried his father. And he ran outside, where he hadn't been for such a long time.

Tom walked outside.
'You know,' said his father. 'There were animals
inside. But they didn't do a thing!'

'That's right,' said Tom.
That was the beginning of
'TOM THE TAMER'S CIRCUS OF PAWS,
CLAWS, BEAKS & BUGS'.
It soon toured the whole garden. And Tom's father
never missed a single show again.

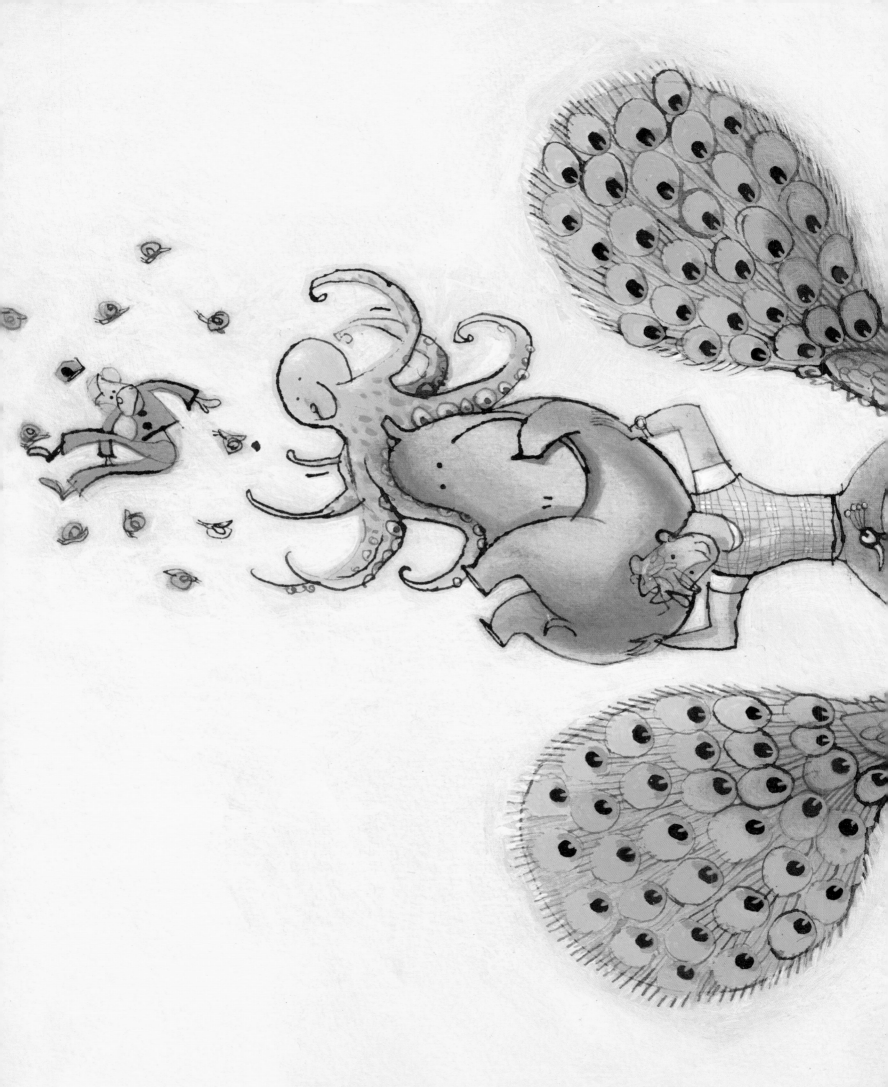